THE
CALL OF THE WILD

Library of Congress Cataloging-in-Publication Data

Hitchner, Earle.
    Call of the wild / by Jack London; retold by Earle Hitchner;
illustrated by Marie De John.
       p.   cm.—(Troll illustrated classics)
    Summary: The adventures of an unusual dog, part St. Bernard, part
Scotch shepherd, forcibly taken to Alaska where he eventually
becomes the leader of a wolf pack.
    ISBN 0-8167-1863-6 (lib. bdg.)   ISBN 0-8167-1864-4 (pbk.)
    1. Dogs—Juvenile fiction. [1. Dogs—Fiction. 2. Wolves—
Fiction. 3. Alaska—Fiction.] I. De John, Marie, ill.
II. London, Jack, 1876-1916. Call of the wild. III. Title.
PZ10.3.H63Cal 1990
[Fic]—dc20   89-33890

Printed in the United States of America.
10 9 8 7 6 5 4 3 2

THE
CALL OF THE WILD

JACK LONDON

Retold by
Earle Hitchner

Illustrated by
Marie De John

Troll Associates

It was the fall of 1897, and the air was filled with the excitement of gold. From all over the world men came seeking the precious yellow metal. They rushed into the Northwest Territories, extending as far as the frozen Alaskan region. All of them hoped to get rich quickly, and sleds pulled by teams of dogs were their primary means of transportation. These dogs had to be big and strong to pull the heavy sleds and thickly furred to withstand the bitter cold.

But Buck knew none of this. He lived happily on Judge Miller's ranch in sunny Santa Clara Valley. The only duties Buck had to perform were to hunt and swim and roll in the grass and accompany the judge's daughters on their morning walks. Among all the dogs housed there, Buck was the leader. His father was a huge St. Bernard, while his mother was a Scotch shepherd dog. Though not as large as his father, Buck weighed an imposing 140 pounds. He had hardened muscles and little fat.

So it never crossed Buck's mind that something was terribly wrong when one of Judge Miller's helpers put a rope around his neck and led him off the ranch one day. Buck thought they were out for a stroll. He realized they weren't when they came to the railroad station. There, the helper handed over the rope to a stranger, who gave him money in return. Buck had no idea that the helper needed the money to pay off a debt.

Buck growled menacingly. And when the stranger jerked the rope tightly around his neck, the dog sprang at him. But the man twisted the rope and threw Buck over on his back. The rope choked Buck, cutting off his breath. Never in his life had Buck been so cruelly treated. He was furious. But his strength ebbed and his eyes glazed. When two other men took hold of his rope leash and threw him into the baggage car of the train, Buck was barely aware of what was happening to him.

The wheels of the train clacked along the rails. Ahead of him, Buck could hear the shrill whistle of the engine. Buck waited for his tormentors to face him again. When they did, he tried to attack them. But they threw him down hard on the baggage car floor and choked him repeatedly until he blacked out.

When Buck awoke, dazed and in pain, he was in a shed. Two men shoved him into a crate. His pride hurt, his throat and tongue burning, Buck lay there in misery. What did these men want with him? Why were they keeping him pent up in this crate?

During the next two days, Buck was given no food or water. Hunger and thirst made him rage inside as he was carted around. First, a wagon carried him, then a ferry steamer, and then another railroad car. The only good thing about this entire journey was that the rope was finally removed. Buck swore no one would ever get another rope around his neck.

The trip ended in the walled backyard of a stout man wearing a red sweater. In his right hand he was holding a club. Without hesitating, the man opened the crate Buck was in.

Buck had never seen a club before, and so he immediately lunged at the man. Buck's eyes were bloodshot and fired with anger. His mouth foamed.

Just as he was about to close his jaws on the man's throat, Buck received a midair blow that forced his teeth to shut in wincing pain. He whirled over and hit the ground with a heavy thud. With a snarl, Buck was on his feet again and leaping at the man. And again, a blow came, bringing him crashing to the ground. A dozen more times he charged, and each time the club broke the charge and smashed him down.

Blood was flowing from Buck's nose and mouth and ears. Buck struggled to his feet, but was too dazed to rush the man again. As Buck stood there limply, the man came toward him and deliberately dealt him a frightful blow on the nose. The pain was incredible.

Enraged, Buck tried one last attack. But the man caught him squarely under the jaw with the club and sent Buck into a midair somersault. Once more, Buck crashed to the ground. Then the man stood over the now helpless dog and struck one last fierce blow that knocked Buck completely unconscious.

7

By the time Buck regained his senses, the man in the red sweater was patting him on the head. "You've learned your place, and I know mine," he said in a friendly voice. "Be a good dog, and all will go well with you. Be a bad dog, and I'll whale the stuffing out of you. Understand?"

The man brought over some water, which Buck lapped up eagerly. Then he gave Buck a generous chunk of meat, which the dog took from the man's hand. Buck knew he was beaten, but not broken. He also knew that he stood no chance against a man with a club. The man with the club was a lawgiver, a master to be obeyed. It was a lesson Buck never forgot.

Not long afterward, a little man visited the yard where Buck was kept. He spoke with the man in the red sweater.

"That's one big bully of a dog you got there," said the little man, his eyes fixed on Buck. "How much?"

"Three hundred," said the man wearing the red sweater. "And seeing it's government money you're spending, Perrault, you shouldn't make any kick about the price."

Perrault smiled. He knew that the cost of good sled dogs had risen sharply in the last few months. And his job as mail carrier for the region would be made easier by a dog as big and powerful as Buck. Perrault gladly paid the three hundred dollars. In return, the man with the red sweater gave him Buck as well as a good-natured Newfoundland dog named Curly.

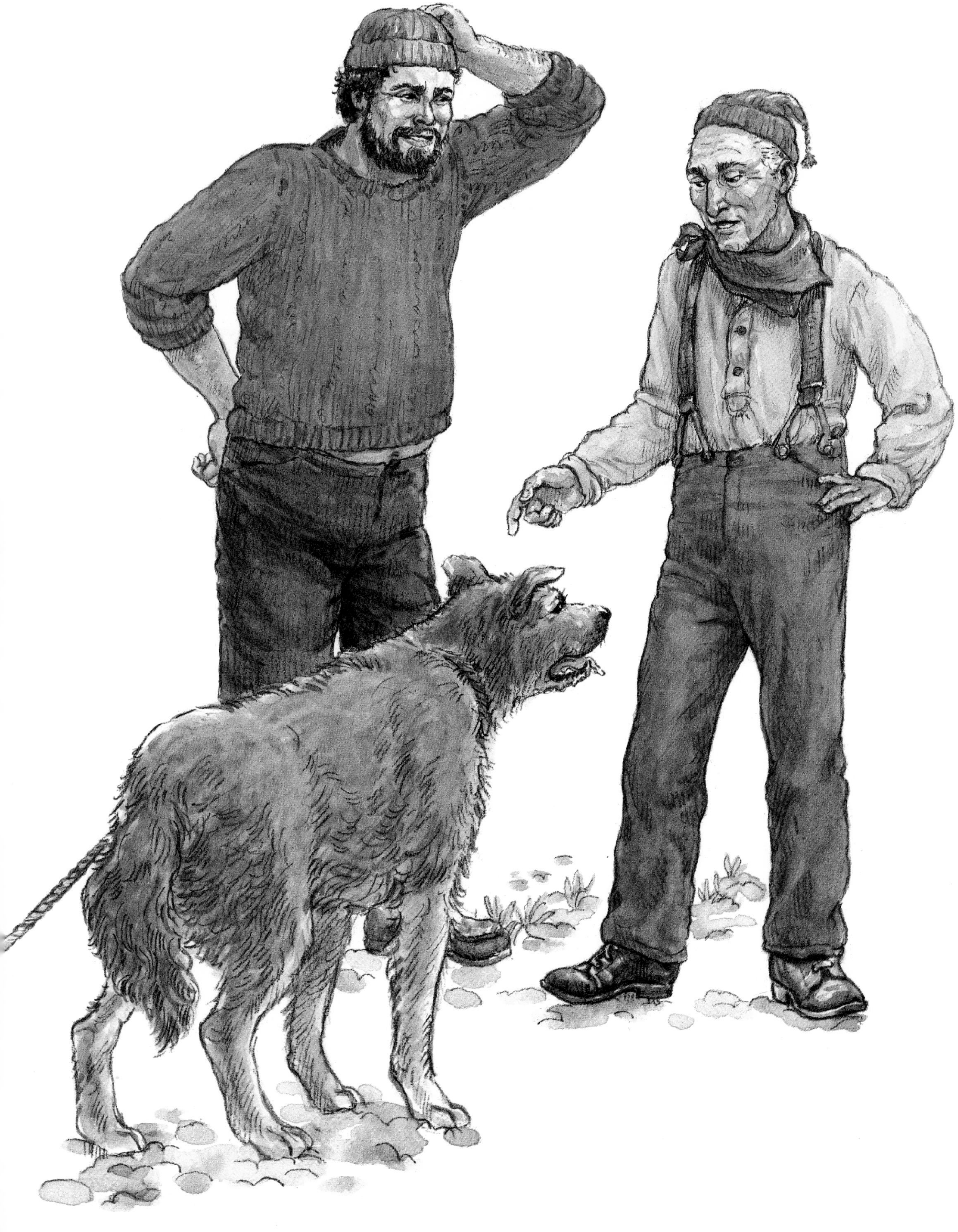

Perrault took the two dogs aboard a ship that was about to head north. A giant of a man named Francois took hold of the dogs and brought them below. There, Buck and Curly joined two other dogs. One, named Dave, bothered no one. The other, called Spitz, was a big, snow-white animal that had once been owned by a whaling captain. He seemed friendly. But Buck soon learned how treacherous Spitz was when he stole from Buck's food at the first meal. Buck sprang at Spitz. But before he could bite the other dog, Francois' whip lashed at Spitz's back in punishment. Buck and Spitz growled at each other. The two were enemies now.

The wind seeping through the cracks in the ship's hold told Buck that the weather was getting colder and colder. Then, Francois came down and leashed all four dogs. He brought them up on deck. Buck blinked his eyes at what he saw. The sky was full of white stuff. When Buck put his foot on deck, it sank into more of the same. It was mushy like mud, yet white. And the more Buck shook the white stuff off his body, the faster it seemed to fall on him. He licked some of it up on his tongue, but in an instant it was gone. This puzzled him. Francois and Perrault laughed at him.

10

"First snow, Buck, eh?" said Francois, still laughing. "Well, get used to it. There's plenty more where we're going."

Snow? Buck now knew that the warmth and peace he had left behind would be his no more. Cold air blasted him in the face as the men stepped down off the boat after it docked. And the dogs Buck saw ashore were like no others he had ever seen. They were savage, scowling beasts, almost wolfish. Buck quickly found out *how* savage when he watched what happened to poor Curly.

The four dogs from the ship were resting by the log store. Curly, in her friendly way, tried to nuzzle a nearby husky the size of a full-grown wolf. Without warning, the husky wheeled on Curly and bit her face. Hardly a second passed before thirty or forty huskies formed a tight circle around Curly and the other dog. Curly rushed her attacker, who again bit her and then stepped aside. The next rush Curly made was met by the other dog's chest. Curly was knocked hard to the ground.

This was what the circle of huskies was waiting for. In a flash, all of them pounced on Curly. She was buried beneath a mass of snarling, yelping dogs. By the time Francois had clubbed them off her, Curly was dead.

The man in the red sweater had taught Buck the law of the club. Curly's death taught Buck the law of the fang. Buck would expect no fair play here in the North. Once down, that would be the end of him. Then Buck caught sight of Spitz, who had enjoyed watching the killing. Spitz was laughing. Buck hated the dog as he had never hated anything or anyone before.

It wasn't long before Buck learned his role in the team of dogs pulling Perrault and Francois' mail sled. "Ho" meant stop. "Mush" meant go. The remaining dogs made sure the lesson sunk in. Every time Buck faltered or made a mistake, Dave nipped his hindquarters. And from the way Spitz barked and cowed and thrashed the other dogs, Buck knew who ruled the team.

Among the dogs in harness with Buck, Dave, and Spitz was Sol-leks. He was a long, gaunt husky with just one eye. He asked nothing, gave nothing, and expected nothing. Sol-leks did not like to be approached from his blind side either. Buck discovered this when his shoulder was slashed by Sol-leks from that side. Even Spitz left Sol-leks alone.

The other dogs in the team were two brothers, Joe and Billee. They were huskies like Sol-leks. Billee was gentle and fun-loving, while his brother, Joe, was surly and hostile. When Perrault and Francois added three more huskies, named Pike, Dub, and Dolly, the team was complete with nine dogs.

In the beginning, the nine dogs pulled the mail sled an average of forty miles a day. But that was over an already packed-down trail. The going became much slower when the dogs had to make their own trail through drifts of freshly fallen snow.

The routine was both simple and demanding: Wake before dawn, pull in harness all day, make camp after dark, eat a meal of sundried fish, then crawl off to sleep in the snow. It was a grueling life, pulling the sled piled heavy with mail over dozens of snow-covered miles. But Buck adapted to it quickly. He had no choice.

And as Buck grew even stronger and hardened to ordinary pain, he grew in cunning and stealth. But all the while, something stirred within him, something untamed. This feeling became so strong in Buck one night that he pointed his nose to the stars and shattered the stillness with a long, wolflike howl. It echoed for miles across the frozen plain. Somehow, in that moment of howling, Buck felt the surge of his ancestors within him.

14

The bad blood between Spitz and Buck deepened as the team continued along the trail. And it might have come to a final death fight the evening Perrault and Francois made camp near a wall of rocks. Buck had made his bed just under a ledge. There, he'd be sheltered from the driving snow and whipping Arctic wind. So snug and warm was his bed that Buck left it reluctantly to get his ration of fish.

When he returned from his meal, Buck found Spitz lying in his bed by the rocks. Up until now, Buck had tried to avoid trouble with his enemy. But this was too much. With all his weight and strength, Buck sprang at Spitz. Spitz just barely managed to dodge Buck's lunge. Soon, the two snarling dogs circled one another, each looking for a weak spot to strike at.

Then, the unexpected happened. A cry from Perrault near the campfire pierced the night. It was followed by the hollow sounds of clubs beating upon bony frames. This, in turn, was followed by squeals of anguish. The camp had been overrun by skulking, growling forms. Ribs clearly showed through their fur. A pack of nearly a hundred starving huskies had picked up the scent of food from the camp and descended on it in force!

Perrault and Francois clubbed them mercilessly. But the blows seemed to have no effect at all. The famished dogs tore into anything that even looked like food, including some of the leather harnesses. Their eyes blazed bright red, and thick white foam bubbled around their muzzles.

When the team dogs were roused from their beds, the invading pack of dogs attacked them. Though they fought bravely, the team dogs were no match for these hunger-crazed huskies. Dave and Sol-leks fought side by side, each dripping blood from multiple wounds. Billee was weeping nearby, while brother Joe was snapping his jaws like a demon.

Buck couldn't believe his eyes. These huskies were terrifying. They meant to destroy anything getting between them and a meal. Once he realized what was happening, Buck broke off his fight with Spitz and ran to help the others. But halfway there, Buck's path was blocked by three huskies. They slashed his head and shoulders. Still, Buck managed to attack one of them. Not wasting a second, Buck leapt at another dog. But at the same time, Buck felt the teeth of another dog at his own throat. It was Spitz, attacking Buck from the side!

16

Buck wrestled free from Spitz's attack and, with the other team dogs, retreated into a forest. Not one team dog escaped with fewer than four or five wounds. Dub was badly injured in a hind leg, Dolly had a torn throat, Joe had lost an eye, and Billee had an ear chewed to ribbons. Only when the pack of roving huskies had left the camp did the team dogs return to it.

Perrault and Francois were in a bad temper. Half the food supply had been devoured. They still had four hundred miles of trail ahead of them, and a cold snap was coming on. Already the thermometer had dropped to fifty degrees below zero—and it was still dropping. To make matters worse, Dolly suddenly went mad, and Francois was forced to kill her.

The hatred between Buck and Spitz had never been more obvious than now. Buck did not forget Spitz's cowardly attack earlier. The two barked and gnashed their teeth in each other's presence. The final showdown between them was drawing closer and closer.

Then, one night after supper, Dub stumbled upon a snowshoe rabbit. It immediately took off from its hiding place in the snow, and all the team dogs chased after it. Even the huskies from a Northwest Police camp nearby heard the team dogs in full cry and joined them in the chase. The rabbit sped down toward the river and turned off into a small frozen creek. It ran lightly on the snow, while the dogs plowed through by strength alone.

Buck led the pack, now sixty dogs strong. His splendid body flashed forward, leap by leap, in the pale moonlight. Still, the rabbit kept a safe distance in front of the dogs. Then Spitz veered off from the pack and cut across a narrow stretch of land. Buck and the other dogs soon found out why. Just ahead of the fleeing rabbit jumped Spitz, cutting off its escape. The moment of hesitation by the rabbit was all that Spitz required to crack its back in midair with his teeth. The pack, seeing the rabbit slain, began to bellow in triumph.

Buck did not join the victory chorus. Instead, he kept running and plowed directly into Spitz. The two spilled over into the powdery snow. Spitz regained his feet in an instant, slashing Buck's shoulder and then leaping clear. The pack, having made short work of the rabbit, ringed the two enemies. The time had come. This fight would be to the death.

Spitz was a veteran battler. He had held sway over all kinds of dogs, and he was clever. He never rushed unless he was prepared to receive a rush. He never attacked unless he knew he could defend against an attack.

In vain, Buck tried to sink his teeth into Spitz's neck, but each time Spitz countered with a bite of his own. Fang rasped against fang, and each dog's lips were cut and bleeding. No matter how hard he tried, Buck could not get through his enemy's guard.

Then Buck changed his tactics. He continued to rush right at Spitz. But at the last moment, instead of going for the dog's throat, Buck would try to drive his shoulder into him and knock him down. But Spitz was ready for the maneuver and slashed Buck each time he tried it. Blood was streaming from Buck now, and he was panting hard. Spitz seemed almost untouched. The circle of dogs tightened around them. They were waiting impatiently to finish off whichever one would fall.

As Buck grew more and more winded, Spitz changed his tactics. He sensed victory was at hand, and he started rushing at Buck, hoping to knock him over. Once, Spitz succeeded, and Buck tumbled into the snow. The whole circle of sixty dogs started up. But Buck recovered in a flash and the circle backed off to wait again.

Buck's strength was nearly spent, while Spitz appeared to be gaining more. Buck knew he couldn't last much longer unless he found a way to trip Spitz up. Then an idea occurred to him. Buck rushed at Spitz once more. He knew Spitz expected him to fake a throat lunge and then try another shoulder plow. But just at the moment when Spitz was ready to slash down at him to ward off the shoulder plow, Buck swept low to the snow and closed his teeth on Spitz's left foreleg. A loud snap could be heard by all the dogs in the circle. Spitz's left front leg was now useless!

The shock and agony on Spitz's face told all. He turned to face Buck on just three legs. Three more times Buck rushed at him, trying the shoulder plow. All three times Spitz eluded him. Then Buck swept low again, breaking Spitz's right foreleg. Despite the pain and helplessness, Spitz still kept his footing. But he saw the circle of dogs tightening ever more closely.

Buck was relentless. Mercy was a thing reserved for gentler times. He sized up his enemy for what would be the final rush at him. Buck could feel the hot breaths of the other dogs on his flanks. They were all in a crouch, waiting to spring. An eerie quiet fell. The only sound was that of Spitz half-growling, half-groaning, as he staggered back and forth.

Like a shot, Buck hurled himself at Spitz. His shoulder crashed into Spitz's, knocking the crippled dog onto his back. The circle of huskies needed no other signal to strike. They sprang on top of the hapless Spitz, who swiftly disappeared underneath them. Buck stood and watched. He was champion, the true leader.

When the team dogs returned to camp, Perrault and Francois saw that Spitz was missing. The wounds covering Buck's body were proof enough of what must have happened to the former lead dog.

"That Spitz must have fought like the devil!" exclaimed Perrault, gazing at Buck's wounds.

"And that Buck must have fought like *two* devils!" replied Francois in admiration. "Now we should make good time. No more Spitz, no more trouble."

When Francois started to harness the dogs in front of the sled, however, Buck went to the front of the team. This surprised the man.

"Get back where you belong, Buck," ordered Francois, cuffing the dog. Buck refused to budge.

Francois grabbed Buck by the scruff of the neck and yanked him backward. Buck growled as Francois placed Sol-leks in the front of the sled. As soon as the man's back was turned, Buck chased Sol-leks from the lead position. Now Francois was angry.

"By gad, I'll fix you!" he shouted, coming toward Buck with a heavy club in his hand.

Buck recalled the man in the red sweater and slowly retreated. The law of the club was as strong as the law of the fang, and Buck never forgot either. He backed away, then circled the camp without coming close enough to be caught and hauled to his former place in harness. Francois and Perrault called out to him to take his old position. But Buck ignored their commands. The lead slot was his by right. He earned it, and he would accept nothing less.

An hour passed, with Perrault and Francois alternately pleading with and cursing at Buck to come back. Time was slipping by fast. The two men knew they should have been on the trail a while ago. Finally, shrugging his shoulders, Francois went over to Sol-leks in the front of the harness, unfastened it, and guided Sol-leks back to his old position. With all the dogs in harness now, only the lead place remained vacant. Francois yelled out to Buck, but still the dog wouldn't come near the sled.

''Throw down the club, Francois,'' advised Perrault.

Francois threw it down. And with head held high, Buck trotted back to the sled. He swung in front of it, taking his place at the head of the team. Francois cried, ''Mush,'' and the sled bounded forward, with Buck setting a fast pace for the team.

It was a record run they made. When the sled pulled into the mining town of Skagway fourteen days later, the team had traveled over 560 miles. For three days, Perrault and Francois puffed out their chests proudly in town. Men clapped them on the back, congratulating them on the record. Others looked on the team dogs with envy.

The celebration didn't last long, however. On the fourth day in town, Perrault and Francois got new orders. Another mail carrier would be taking over the team dogs and sled. After reading the orders, Francois went over to Buck and threw his arms around him. Perrault did the same. Both whispered something in Buck's ear that the dog had never heard before: ''Goodbye.''

The man who replaced Perrault and Francois hitched up the team dogs and traveled the same trail. But the mail sled the dogs pulled this time was much heavier than before. The routine didn't change: Wake before sunrise, work past sundown, eat, sleep. The work was back-breaking, and one day blurred into another. Their team was one among a dozen others along the trail. But Buck quickly established himself as leader over all the dogs.

At night, once he finished his portion of fish, Buck liked to lie near the campfire. He stretched out his forelegs, basking in the fire's warm glow. Sometimes Buck dreamed of Judge Miller's big house in Santa Clara Valley. It was so long ago and far away that it seemed he had never lived there at all. Other times, Buck remembered the man in the red sweater, the death of Curly, and the great fight with Spitz. But these memories and dreams dimmed beside another, stronger feeling. It was what made him howl at the moon and the stars at night. It was what made him want to run free through the woods. He tried to shake this feeling, but it refused to leave him.

Buck felt a slight jolt to his ribcage. Waking, he sensed it was just before dawn. The driver was peering down at him.

''C'mon, Buck,'' he said. ''We've a lot of miles ahead of us yet.''

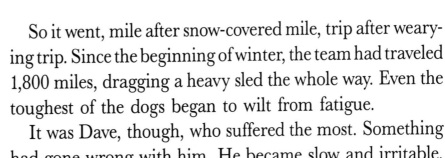

So it went, mile after snow-covered mile, trip after wearying trip. Since the beginning of winter, the team had traveled 1,800 miles, dragging a heavy sled the whole way. Even the toughest of the dogs began to wilt from fatigue.

It was Dave, though, who suffered the most. Something had gone wrong with him. He became slow and irritable. If the harness jerked suddenly, he would cry out in pain. The driver examined him and found nothing physically wrong. Yet Dave cried out each time he was prodded to join the team in harness.

Not one to shirk his duty, Dave tried with all his might to keep up with the other dogs. But more and more he was lagging behind. He was getting weaker and weaker, but he would not allow the driver to take him out of the harness. His pride remained as strong as ever. No matter how much pain he felt, Dave insisted on pulling his share of the load. But it became plain to all that he couldn't anymore.

One morning, with the other dogs already in harness, Dave could not rise up on his legs. He lay gasping in the snow. Tears ran down his cheeks at the sight of the sled pulling forward without him. Soon the team dogs could hear Dave howling mournfully behind them.

When the team drew close to a belt of river timber, the driver halted the sled and walked back in the direction where Dave was. A revolver shot rang out. In the same split second, Dave's howling stopped. The driver came back hurriedly and shouted the team forward. The sled plowed ahead. But Buck knew, as every dog in harness knew, what had just taken place.

By the time the team pulled into Skagway, they were in a wretched state, worn down and worn out. Buck's 140-pound body had shrunk to just 115 pounds. The rest of the team dogs were no better off than he. Pike and Sol-leks were both limping badly, while Dub was aching from a wrenched shoulder blade. All of the dogs were footsore. Every muscle and every fiber of their bodies twinged in pain. Over the last 1,800 miles, they had received only five days' rest. Once the sled stopped in town, the team crumpled to the ground.

The long rest they needed and expected, however, was not to come. The driver got new orders to take out a fully-harnessed team in four days. A fresh batch of Hudson Bay dogs was to replace the old team. Those dogs no longer able to work would be gotten rid of. The others were to be sold.

On the morning of the fourth day, with Buck and the other team dogs still exhausted, the mail carrier sold them to two men. One was named Charles, a middle-aged man with weak eyes and a drooping lower lip. The other was named Hal. He was nineteen or twenty years old and seemed quick to anger. He carried a big Colt revolver on a belt loaded with bullets. He also had a hunting knife tucked in his belt. The fresh, untested look on both men's faces showed Buck how out of place they were in this northern territory. Instinctively, Buck distrusted them.

When driven with the rest of the team to their new owners' camp, Buck was shocked at what he saw. Their tent was barely standing erect, the ground was strewn with unwashed dishes, and everything was a mess. Out of the teetering tent popped a woman called Mercedes by the men. She was Charles' wife and Hal's sister, Buck learned. All three of them seemed totally incapable of coping with each other, let alone the frozen wilderness they'd be entering. Buck feared for the future of the team in such clumsy hands.

The way the three loaded the sled confirmed Buck's impression of them. Dishes were packed unwashed, bundles of unneeded clothing were stacked lopsided, and the huge tent was sloppily folded and placed on top. All the while, Mercedes constantly gave orders to the two men. She would tell them to move a bundle to the front of the sled, then seconds later order them to move it back again. The result was a top-heavy sled with its runners sunk deeply into the snow.

''Mush!'' shouted Hal, cracking a whip. ''Mush on there!''

The dogs sprang forward, only to be stopped dead by the taut pull of the harness. They strained and strained, but the sled held firm.

"Lazy brutes, I'll show you!" cried Hal, furious. But as he was about to flog the dogs with his whip, Mercedes raised her hand for him to stop.

"Oh, Hal, you mustn't," she said. "The poor dears! Promise me you won't be harsh with them for the rest of the trip. Otherwise, I won't go a step."

"Precious lot you know about dogs," he sneered. "They're lazy, I tell you. A good whipping is how you get them to obey. That's their way. Ask any of the men here."

The spectacle of these three trying to get their sled moving had attracted quite a few bystanders. One of them spoke up.

"They're weak as water," said the bystander. "Plumb tuckered out, that's what's the matter with them. They need a rest."

But Mercedes stuck up for her brother. "Never mind him, Hal. You're driving the dogs. You do what you think is best with them."

Once more, Hal's whip lashed out at the dogs. Once more, the dogs dug in and strained against the harness. And once more, the sled stood still as if it were an anchor. Two more efforts produced the same result. The dogs stood there panting as the whip cracked over their heads and against their flanks. Then Mercedes got off the sled and dropped on her knees before Buck.

"Why won't you pull hard?" she asked him. "Then you won't get whipped." Buck just looked at her blankly.

Another bystander spoke up. "It's not that I care a whoop about what happens to the three of you, but for the dogs' sake, break out the runners from the ice. If you throw your weight from side to side, they should work free."

Hal followed his advice. As the dogs strained one more time against the harness, he threw his body sharply from side to side. The ice holding the sled's runners crackled underneath, then the runners slipped out. The sled was finally away. But halfway down the town's main street, where it curved, the sled toppled over. And the dogs never stopped pulling. They were still angry about being whipped. All the belongings on the sled scattered along the street as the dogs raced ahead, ignoring Hal's shouts of "Whoa!"

Some kindhearted citizens took the three new owners aside and told them what they'd need for the journey ahead. Half the load and twice the dogs—that was the advice the three got. And so they lightened the load by half, and went out and bought six new dogs for the harness. At last, with no further delay or mishap, they were on their way.

The slushy snow and cracked ice beneath the dogs' feet told them spring was coming. Small pools of water collected on the surface of once completely frozen streams. Not only did this make traveling slower and more difficult, it also made it dangerous. The trail could give way at any time now. But the three owners continued on, arguing among themselves all the while, ignoring the danger signs around them.

To get the dogs to pull even faster, Hal decided to double their rations of food. What he didn't give them and what they sorely needed was rest. So the dogs made poor time as their strength waned. Only a quarter of the journey had been covered by the time Hal woke up to the fact that half the dog food had already been eaten. And so he cut all the dogs' rations and tried to increase each day's travel.

Dub was the first dog to drop, and Hal promptly shot him with the Colt he was carrying. In quick succession, the six new dogs dropped from hunger and exhaustion. Hal used his revolver to put each out of his misery. The team had nearly been halved by overwork and underfeeding, slowing progress even more. The bickering among the three owners grew shriller.

Hal was especially gruff. Mercedes and Charles had persuaded him to give his prized revolver to an old Indian woman they met along the trail. In exchange, she gave them a few pounds of frozen horsehide to feed the dogs. The dogs tore off the horsehide in strips and swallowed them whole. It was a poor substitute for real food, but it was all they had to eat now.

Billee, good-natured to the end, died next. It seemed a short time before the team was down to just five dogs. Buck led as usual, though with no heart or pride in his work. All five of the dogs were like walking skeletons. Their ribs showed through their coats. With Mercedes weeping, Hal cursing, Charles muttering, and the dogs failing, the sled staggered into the camp of John Thornton at the mouth of the White River.

After only a brief rest, Hal, Mercedes, and Charles prepared to set out on the trail again. But Buck would go no farther. The team had been lucky to make it to this point. Buck knew their luck would not hold out much longer.

''Get up there, Buck!'' Hal commanded. ''Get up! Mush on!''

34

Buck made no effort to move. Hal whipped him and the other dogs, who struggled to their feet. Buck still lay on the ground. The whip cut into his flanks again and again. Hal was in a rage now. He dropped the whip, took up a club, and started beating Buck with it. Blow upon blow thundered down on him, but Buck refused to stir. Buck was nearly numb past pain when the camp owner himself, John Thornton, suddenly barreled into Hal. The driver sprawled headlong onto the ground.

"Strike that dog one more time," shouted Thornton, "and I'll kill you!"

"It's my dog," replied Hal, wiping the blood from his mouth, which he had cut in the fall. "Get out of my way, or I'll fix you, too!"

Hal pulled out his hunting knife and came at Thornton with it. But before Hal got too close, Thornton kicked the knife from Hal's hand, then knocked him down with a single punch. Hal was still on the ground when Thornton went over to the harness and cut Buck loose from it.

All the fight was gone from Hal. Feeling Buck was as good as dead anyway, Hal jumped on the sled and headed it out over the river. Thornton turned away from the departing sled and examined Buck's coat for broken bones. But all he found were the ugly red welts left by the whip, some deep bruises, and signs of terrible hunger.

A sharp, crackling sound made Thornton turn around and look out onto the river. There, he saw the back end of the sled drop down into the ice. A moment later, a whole section of river ice disappeared. With it went the sled, the remaining team dogs, and the three owners. Their screams ripped through the wind blowing off the river, then were heard no more.

John Thornton and Buck looked at each other. ''You poor devil,'' said Thornton to Buck, who licked his hand.

Not even on Judge Miller's ranch in Santa Clara Valley had Buck ever received kinder treatment. John Thornton warmed his feet, fed him, stroked his fur, and nursed him back to health. The sheen returned to Buck's thick coat. And for the first time, Buck felt genuine *love* for his master.

John Thornton had saved his life, had taken care of him, and was an ideal owner. He had a way of taking Buck's head and shaking it between his hands that made Buck's heart leap. Buck would respond by gently taking Thornton's hand between his teeth and holding it without biting it. They were playful together, and the love they had for each other only strengthened over time.

Thornton's two dogs, Skeet and Nib, were unlike any dogs Buck had met in the frozen North. They were friendly toward him and showed no jealousy. Skeet, an Irish setter, had even helped Thornton restore Buck's health by cleaning Buck's fur with her tongue. Nib was a huge black dog, half bloodhound, half deerhound. He had eyes that laughed and a nature as good as Skeet's.

37

At long last, Buck felt he had found a master he could trust and love. He had never been so happy. But still, that longing he felt when the moon shone brightly at night never left him. He loved John Thornton, but something stronger than that love silently called to him from the wilderness. When the call became too strong to resist, Buck would leave Thornton's campfire and plunge into the surrounding forest. On and on he'd roam, following his instinct. And only the love he bore for Thornton would eventually draw Buck back to the campfire.

Buck's love for Thornton became so great that he would do anything for him and anything to protect him. Once, standing on the edge of a steep cliff, Thornton jokingly ordered Buck to jump over it. In a flash, Buck was running toward the cliff's edge. He was just about to leap over it when Thornton caught him at the last moment. A shudder went through Thornton. He never gave Buck such a foolish command again.

Another time, in a saloon, an evil man named Burton had picked a quarrel with another man at the bar. Thornton tried to break it up and Burton slugged him. No sooner did Burton's fist connect than Buck leaped at Burton. By the time Buck was pulled off Burton, the man was bleeding heavily from the neck. A doctor was summoned to the saloon and managed to stop the bleeding. From that day forward, Buck's reputation spread among all the local mining camps. This was a dog no one dared anger!

Later on that year, Buck came to John Thornton's rescue
again. This time, Buck saved his master's life. While poling
his boat down the churning rapids of a river, John Thornton
was flung from the boat when it suddenly crashed into some
rocks hidden just below the surface. It was Buck who jumped
into the foaming white water and swam to save him.

Thornton took hold of Buck's neck as the dog pulled him
toward shore. They went under several times, each gasping
for air. The water battered them and threw them against
jagged rocks along the bottom. It took every ounce of Buck's
strength to drag his master onto the riverbank. There, the
two collapsed.

Thornton was nearly drowned, and his body was badly
bruised from the rocks. When he examined Buck's wet,
exhausted body, he discovered three of Buck's ribs had
been broken in the rescue.

News of this latest exploit by Buck also spread among the mining camps. But perhaps nothing compared with what Buck did one wintry day in the town of Dawson. John Thornton, along with his two mining partners, made what would otherwise have been a very foolish bet. They wagered a thousand dollars with another miner that Buck could pull from a dead start a sled carrying a thousand-pound load a hundred yards.

To make matters worse, Thornton and his two partners didn't have the thousand dollars to lose. They were almost flat broke from their last trip in which they had lost most of their supplies in the river rapids. If Buck couldn't pull the sled the required distance, Thornton and his partners would be wiped out.

The miner who accepted their bet spoke up confidently. "I've got a sled standing outside, with twenty sacks of flour weighing fifty pounds each. Let's see if that almighty dog of yours can pull it as you say he can. Right now!"

Word of the bet spread like wildfire among the other townspeople. In minutes, the street was lined with a huge crowd. Other bets could be heard being bandied among the onlookers. Everyone was excited.

Buck was hitched in front of the sled. Thornton knelt down by his head and shook it softly between his hands. "As you love me, Buck," he whispered into the dog's ear. "As you love me." Then Thornton moved away. A hush fell over the crowd.

Standing aside, Thornton yelled, "Now, Buck!" The dog tightened the harness around himself, then slackened it a few inches. Buck knew the runners were frozen solid in the ice. He had to break them out if he had any chance of budging the sled. He lunged to the right, then just as swiftly lunged to the left. The load quivered, and from under the runners arose a crisp, crackling sound.

"Haw!" commanded Thornton.

Buck pulled with all his might. The crackling gave way to a snapping sound. The runners were breaking free and slipping ever so slowly out of their grooves. The sled was moving!

"Now, mush, Buck! MUSH!" shouted Thornton.

His master's command brought a sudden surge of strength to Buck. His whole body tensed under the tremendous load. His muscles writhed and knotted like live things under his silky coat. He kept his chest low to the ground and his head forward and down. The sled swayed and trembled. Then Buck lost his footing. A groan swelled up from the crowd.

Buck paid no heed and regained his feet. He now pulled as hard as he could—harder than even *he* thought he could. The sled moved forward a few inches, then a few feet, and finally a few yards. Thornton was shouting encouragement from behind. Each word from his master gave Buck new energy.

Soon, Buck could see the pile of firewood that was the finish line. He was now a few yards short of it. Cheers from the crowd grew louder and louder in Buck's ears as he moved closer to the finish line. One final burst of strength was all it would take to cross it.

"Buck, you can do it! Just a little farther!" his master urged.

That was all Buck needed. He lunged past the firewood, stopping finally on Thornton's command.

A deafening roar rose up from the surrounding crowd. Hats and mittens and scarves were tossed into the air. Men shook hands with those standing next to them. And Thornton fell on his knees by Buck's head, cradling it in his arms. "You did it, Buck!" he cried, hugging the dog. "You did it!"

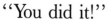

With the money won from the bet, John Thornton and his two partners set out for a mining camp far to the east. It was a region where few men ventured. Thornton had heard of a gold strike there that had been abandoned long ago because of Indian attacks. The three men were determined to find the site and mine it.

The search took longer than expected. Months came and went, the seasons passed, and still no gold strike was in sight. Then, during the second spring of the journey, they came upon an old, spruce-bough lodge by a stream. This was not the place they were looking for. But when the men panned for gold in the stream, they turned up enough bright yellow nuggets and gold dust to fill bag after bag. They stayed there for weeks, panning and packing the gold, then stacking the bags outside the lodge.

Buck and the rest of the team dogs didn't have much to do. Occasionally, they brought back firewood on the sled or hauled back meat freshly killed by the men for food. Most of the time, though, the dogs played and dozed peacefully by the lodge while the men worked the stream.

Buck was the exception. Wild yearnings caused him to leave the camp and explore the wilderness. Each time out was a little longer than the time before. Then, Buck stayed away from camp for a full week.

During that period, Buck ran down through the steep forest slopes. He loved to surprise other animals, using his stealth to creep up on them. He lived off the land, killing only what he needed to eat.

One night that week, Buck met a timber wolf. They approached each other hesitantly at first, each snapping his jaws to keep the other at bay. Finally, the wolf sniffed noses with Buck. Then the two ran side by side through the forest and into a valley. Buck was joyous. He knew he was at last answering the call he had always heard within him. He ran beside his wood brother for countless miles.

Buck was far away from the campsite when he decided to return to it. He started back in an easy lope. But as he came closer to the camp, he stopped and sniffed the air. Something was wrong, and he moved more cautiously. Three miles from the camp, Buck came upon a fresh trail, one not made by the three men. Traveling along it, Buck picked up an unusual scent to the side. He nosed behind some bushes and found Nib. An arrow was sticking out from either side of him. He was dead.

Buck broke into a run toward the camp. He could now hear voices, and they weren't the men's. As he ran, Buck passed the rest of the team dogs. All were lying dead on the ground. Their sides were pierced with many arrows. Then Buck stopped. Before him was a group of Indians dancing and chanting in front of the wreckage of the lodge.

Like a hurricane of fury, Buck hurled himself at the Indians before they knew what had hit them. He sprang at the nearest Indian, killing him. Without hesitating, Buck jumped on another Indian. He was in constant, dizzying motion—biting and tearing. The Indians' arrows were shot at too close a range to do any damage. Soon they were wounding each other with their own arrows!

Buck never stopped, never allowed himself to tire. Even when the Indians finally retreated through the forest, Buck pursued them, dragging many of them down like deer. Of the entire band, only a few Indians escaped with their lives. And those who were still running shrieked in terror about the "evil spirit" that was chasing them in the form of a monstrous dog.

Buck, tired of the chase, returned to the campsite. Thornton's two partners lay dead before the lodge. And further on, by the stream, Buck found his good friend Skeet face down in the water. The proud Irish setter had defended her master with her last breath, for the body of John Thornton lay close beside Skeet's.

Buck let out a long, wailing howl over his fallen master. No greater love existed between man and dog than that between John Thornton and Buck. Now, he was gone from Buck's life forever!

In the years that followed, a new tale was told by the Indians of the region. It was the legend of the Ghost Dog. No creature was more feared. Its strength was the strength of a hundred timber wolves. Its cunning was far greater than any man's.

The Ghost Dog ran proudly at the head of a large wolf pack. Its eyes burned like coals in the moonlight. Its thick muscles and heavy fur rippled as it ran in the wild. And though snug in their tepees, the Indians trembled at night when they could hear the Ghost Dog howling. It was singing the song of the pack. It was answering the call of the wild.